# Pages of the Mind

By
## Students of La Quinta High School
Westminster, California

# Pages of the Mind

ISBN: 978-0-692-73022-5

**Edited and Compiled by:** Amanda LaPera
**Copy Editors:** Jennifer Chau, Monica Van
**Section Editors:** Sadie Adams, Zachary King, Alexandra Quang, Richard Trejo
**Design Editor:** Kari Nguyen
**Cover Designed by:** Kari Nguyen

Published by La Quinta High School Creative Writing Class

# CONTENTS

**Dedicated to the authors yet to come**


## Introduction

This is the next book in our creative writing collection of anthologies. All stories, plays, and poems were written by high school students at La Quinta High School. For many students, this is their first publication. As for our first class of seniors:

> "Parting is such sweet sorrow"
>
> --William Shakespeare, *Romeo and Juliet*

# *FROM THE BACKYARD*

And here lies the oak in the man's backyard

>Desiccated by a sun sitting high beside the Lord

Exhausted out of things to say; say

>Have you seen the trees sway in such a way?

Sickened by this affectual animosity

>This synthetic, manufactured monstrosity borne of hypocrisy

Coagulated from the imperfect forty-six amalgamations-

>23 North from misguided endearments and ill-placed in(at)tentions

The other half South from across the sea by the efforts of self-intervention -

>To save himself from the cold, calculated convention

Designed between whites clad in royal blues and honeyed yellow; my fellow

>Do you not see they are all freshly coated in blood?

All the same crimson shades,

>Scarlet stories painted with swords and sickle blades

Across desert, mountain, and pacific sands

>Painted on flags and told by the people whose' graves upon I stand

With the same fears of a becoming nothing more than a mere bloodstain

>Poured down the technicolored drain because his sprained mind had nothing to
>
>gain

When he couldn't learn from the pain

>His daddy experienced when he lost his sister on the Atlantic Train.

In his mind repeats the definition of insanity

>When at the apotheosis of clarity

The father declares communicative bankruptcy

>To the aspirations of a boy who dreamed of not Oriental prosperity, but charity.

When only half the words of his mouth come out

>When only half the sapling of a great oak tree was beginning to sprout

Only to be stomped by a lack of faith

Under the boot of a patriarchal gardener made irate.

In just a few words a psychological pesticide was administered

To deter any accidental filicide by the still-insecure version of him:

the lesser miniature.

And to ease and coax the fears so that the father's and the son's eyes would stop

dripping tears

The sapling smiled as though it were another's child

Instead, the reminder of hate reiterates as the words are flung out of the mouth

of my Pop:

"Don't let that naive happiness of yours run wild.

Cut the innocence clean and wean off of this happiness

You live in a world so greedy, so gluttonous

Its last and best impressions

Is this sniffling crybaby I've grown here in the US.

Can't you see why I studied, worked to become the best?

Liars and promise-breakers like Ho Chi Minh stole from the rest."

*Vincent Nguyen*

# *IF I TOLD YOU THAT I LOVED YOU, WOULD YOU STAY?*

If I was to tell you that
My undying love for you
Would never leave your side,
Would you believe me?

Even when the tears
Stream down both our faces
While I lightly grasp your hand
Weaving my fingers into yours
As I wish you a final goodbye
For the next four years

The pain of my warmth
Leaves you with remnants of my love
As I slowly make my way
Watching you drive away
From everything I knew
For the last few years

The memories of us
Together for one last time
Will be the things that keep me
Whole
While I wait to see you
Once again

The photos of us
Will remain on my wall
Memories of the good times
Where all we would do was smile
Our world never ending

Even when the late night calls
Aren't good enough anymore
Or the visits always
Seem to go by to fast
My love will always be with you
No matter where we are

Will you still believe
That my love for you
Will never cease
To fade?

*Nancy Le*

# THE SEARCH

The night fell as I lay my head on the pillow
With my thoughts fluttering away

In my dreams, I see you looking at me
With your clear eyes and long hair

I reach out before you leave
And run away from my sight once more

I touched your cheeks, lifting your lips to mine
So soft, warm, and pure: a kiss of vow

My love, I held onto you, onto your heart as
We sing, nightingales at the dawn of spring

I closed my eyes as we say our last goodbyes
You walk away, holding our love, our promise

The morning dew washed me away
I will look for you, search for your love, next night.

*Kari Nguyen*

# *RISE*

Confined in the unconscious
The eerie melody continues to play
A phobia of the past
An invisible chain holds down my conscious
Flying around like lost bird within the darkness
Will anyone hear my miserable heart?
I played a part to fit the crowd's expectations
The shadows around continue to laugh
Am I the only one limping?
I laugh back hysterically,
I will prove them wrong and chain the pain down
Trampled wings will eventually heal
I will steal the win
Failure, frustration
Even with trampled wings, I will not falter
Like a phoenix's revival
I will rise.

*Amy Tran*

# i.

Her feelings bubbled up silently until one day she saw him,
his smile and his crinkled eyes, and her heart said
"oh, I do like him."

He spoke with amusement in his voice and stars in his eyes,
words that she was surprised would come from his mouth.
(you're a lot more mature than I had thought)
Her heart called out to him.

From then on, she watched as he
talked to his friends,
walked slowly to and from the room
laughed until he looked like he would cry.

She did everything she could to get him to glance at her.
Drive miles to see him,
smile in his direction, even if he was not looking.
Speak high praises,
forget the flaws that he obviously had.

it did not come as a surprise to see him smile at other gems.
Jade and diamond are both quite beautiful,
so she'll sit here, watching as he sends hellos to others.

and yes, sometimes she will sit and wonder
why to him, she is not as beautiful and shining like
a diamond or jade,
but she's not foolish enough to say that she is not a gem.

Her heart calls out to him,
and she desperately hopes that one day his heart will do the same.

But for now, the flowers in her heart will bloom against adversity.
The unspoken words that she swallows will be nutrients the flower needs,
and her feelings are the water that gives these flowers the power to survive.

r.c. you may not like her,
but she likes you enough for the seeds in both your lungs to grow.

*Tracey Hoang*

8

# *JAX*

by Zachary King


## CHARACTERS

JAX, *an over-enthusiastic, over-imaginative pre-teen who has a frequent tendency to tell stories that everyone regards as tall tales. Or are they?*
SARAH, *JAX'S mother, who welcomes her son's creativity, even when she is strongly annoyed by it.*
STEVE, *JAX'S father, who just wishes his boy would grow up and stop lying, no matter how ridiculous his excuses are.*
BILLY, *JAX'S best friend*
NATURAL: *A mysterious, ghastly man.*
COPS, *Cops.*


*Scene 1*

(*Curtain rises. We see a small suburban kitchen L, with a table with three seats and a fridge. R should be a living room arrangement, with a couch and coffee table, maybe a few chairs. STEVE and SARAH sitting at the kitchen table drinking coffee, doing generic actions such as typing on a laptop or reading a newspaper. Enter JAX, UR*)

JAX:  (*Out of breath*) Mom, dad, you'll never believe what just happened!

(*Everyone else groans.*)

SARAH:  What is it this time, dear?
JAX:  This guy - he was super creepy; he had red, glowing eyes and long, sharp teeth - he followed me home, but right as I turned up the driveway, he ran away, and I was so scared, and I tried to outrun him, but he was really, really fast, and-
STEVE:  (*Interrupting*) Jax, do you honestly expect us to believe that a man - a vampire, actually - chased you down the street as you were walking home from the park in one of the safest gated communities this side of Springfield?"
JAX:  Yeah, and--
STEVE:  And I suppose this is similar to the dire wolf that ran through the school, hunting you down so it could eat your homework?

9

JAX:     But--

STEVE:     Or the invisible man that you almost caught stealing my wallet off of my nightstand?

JAX:     B--but--

STEVE:     Or maybe this "vampire" is friends with the 60-foot tall ice cream man that forced the school to close down after he flooded it with hot fudge. Jax, you're almost thirteen. It's time to stop this childishness.

SARAH:     (*comforting JAX*) He's right, Jackie. You don't need to pretend everything is from a scary ghost story. The truth is, the world is scary enough as it is. You don't need to pretend it's worse.

JAX:     (*Crying*) I'm sorry, mom, but I was really scared. You and dad and Mrs. Smith all keep telling me not to trust strangers.

SARAH:     I know sweetie. But no one has sharp teeth and red eyes. C'mon.

(*She and JAX enter kitchen. SARAH takes a popsicle out of the freezer. JAX smiles. Blackout*)


Scene 2

(*A bench is placed C. A sign reading "Mulberry Street" stands, DR. NATURAL in a black trench coat and fedora leans against it. Enter JAX and BILLY UL.*)

JAX:     And then I said, 'Yeah, I knocked him out.' (*Punches air*)

BILLY:     Wow, Jax. I wish I was as tough as you.

JAX:     Yeah, bro. Everyone does. But don't worry, if we ever get into a fight, I got your back.

(*Stop and sit on bench. NATURAL approaches them.*)

BILLY:     It's just that, you're really tough, and I'm really wimpy.

JAX:     Don't worry, Bill. Besides, it's not like anyone's gonna actually attack us.

NATURAL: (*Behind bench*) You don't really think that's true, do you?

JAX:     (*Startled*) Who are you?

NATURAL: I am Sir Percival Reginald Natural, at your service.

BILLY:     W-what are you doing here?

NATURAL: I heard you boys have run into some trouble lately with vampires, true?

JAX:     How--

NATURAL: You two walk down one of the most populated suburban streets in this neighborhood. Do you honestly expect people not to hear you?

JAX:     Do you know about vampires?

NATURAL: Yes, of course. They're a plague on this land. I hunt them. (*Reveals a wooden stake and braid of garlic within trench coat. Pulls out notepad.*) I was hoping you'd give me details about this vampire you encountered.

JAX:.     Well, he was tall and had pale skin. His eyes were red and he had really sharp teeth.

NATURAL: All of his teeth were sharp?

JAX:     Yeah, and he was fast. Faster than anything I'd seen before in my life.

NATURAL: Not even a car?

JAX:     Well, faster than any *person,* I guess. But he almost beat me to my house.

NATURAL: Anything else stand out to you? Birthmarks? Scars? Bite marks?

JAX:     He did have two little holes on his neck…

NATURAL: Great. Thank you, young one. I'll look into this at once. Can I get your names, please?

JAX:     Call me Zak. This is my friend Phillip.

NATURAL: A pleasure to meet you both. I must be off now.(*Starts L*)

JAX:     Wait, one more thing. (*NATURAL stops.*) He had a dark red parasol.

NATURAL: (*Tips fedora*) Thank you, child. I'll be in the neighborhood if you want to join me on my mission.

JAX:     I dunno if my mom'll let me.

NATURAL: There are some things you don't need to ask permission for, Zak. I'll be waiting.

JAX:     Wait! Maybe you can convince my mom to let me go with you.

NATURAL: That would be fine, child. But you must swear to follow my instructions to a T if you are to hunt with me.

JAX: Okay, as long as I get to hunt monsters!

(*Blackout*)


*Scene 3*
(*Back at the house. SARAH sits on couch on a laptop. Enter JAX UR.*)

JAX:     Mom, mom!

SARAH:     (*Sighs*) What is it this time, Jax?

JAX:     Me and Billy were walking home, and this scary guy in a trench coat said that he'd hunt down that vampire and kill him!

SARAH:       A guy in a trench coat?

JAX:     Yeah, he had a wooden stake, and--

SARAH:     Jax, it's very dangerous to talk to strangers. You didn't even know this guy.

JAX:     He told us his name. Sir Natural. He even said 'at your service.'

11

SARAH:   That doesn't exempt him from being a predator. Jax, I've told you a thousand times, don't talk to strangers.

JAX:   But he hunts vampires, mom.

SARAH:   (*Shouting*) Vampires don't exist, Jax. (*Pause, calmly*) Honey, this needs to stop.

(*JAX stomps DR, and SARAH goes back to sitting with laptop. A doorbell rings.*)

SARAH:   Coming!

(*SARAH mimics opening a door UL, and NATURAL forces his way in.*)

NATURAL: Good evening, madam. I am Sir Percival Reginald Natural, at your--

SARAH:   Get out.

NATURAL: I'm sorry?

SARAH:   My son told me about you. You stay away from my son. Stay away from Billy, and stay away from this neighborhood, Natural. If that's even your real name.

NATURAL: I don't understand, I--

SARAH:   Then let me make it perfectly clear. (*Punches his face*) Get. Out.

NATURAL (*Rubbing cheek*): If you would just let me explain--

(*SARAH elbows him in the gut. He runs off UL. She shakes her hands as JAX enters UR*)

JAX:   Mom, was that--

SARAH:   Go to your room.

JAX:   But that sounded like--

SARAH:   Room. Now.

(*JAX runs past her and exits UL*)

Jax, you get back here this instant. Jax? Jax!

(*Exits UL. Blackout*)


*Scene 4*

(*The house again, the next day. Two policemen stand over SARAH and STEVE, who are at dining table. SARAH cries throughout scene, with STEVE comforting her.*)

SARAH:   He was tall. Wore a black trench coat and fedora, I didn't get a good

12

look at his face.

COP 1:    And you say your son met this man before?

SARAH:    Yes, Jax said he was a vampire hunter. Wooden stake and everything.

COP 2:    And do you know a Billy LeMar?

SARAH:    Yes, he was Jax's best friend.

COP 2:    He was found dead last night in a gutter. Had a huge, open wound in his heart.

COP 1:    And that's all you could tell us, ma'am?

SARAH:    Yes.

COP 1:    Alright then. (*COP 2 Exits UL.*) We'll keep an eye out for your son. I'd invest in some child-proof locks. (*Exits*)

STEVE:    You realize that we'll have to tell him, right?

SARAH:    It can wait. We'll wait until he's an adult.

STEVE:    No, we won't. Sarah, we've been lying to him for almost thirteen years. It's time to let the truth come out.

SARAH:    (*Looks up at STEVE. After a long pause*) I'll do it.

STEVE:    (*Sniffs, then, after another pause*) You smell him, don't you?

SARAH:    Of course. I'm his mother.

STEVE:    Let's go, then.

(*Blackout*)


*Scene 5*

(*Street corner with sign and bench. JAX lies on bench, hands tied, surrounded by cloves of garlic. NATURAL, now in a suit with a bottle of water, leans over him from behind.*)


NATURAL: What did this vampire look like again?

JAX:    He had a dark red parasol.

NATURAL: Like this? (*Pulls out parasol*)

JAX:    You're -you're a-

NATURAL: No, I'm not, Jax. I found this in your house, right next to you front door.

JAX:    But, I'm not a--

NATURAL: (*Sprinkles water on JAX, who flinches slightly*) You're stubborn, vampire. I'm impressed. I've killed many of your kind before, but none were as resilient as you.

JAX:    I'm not a vampire. I'm twelve.

NATURAL: Lies.

SARAH:    (*Off R*) How dare you call my son a liar.


(*SARAH runs on, jumps on NATURAL, and bites his neck. The two struggle as STEVE begins untying JAX. STEVE picks up parasol and whacks NATURAL in the head, knocking him out.*)

| | |
|---|---|
| STEVE: | You bit him? |
| SARAH: | Figured that he couldn't fight us if he joined us. |
| JAX: | What's going on? |
| SARAH: | Go throw that garlic away, Jax. That stuff's poison. |

(*Blackout*)

*Scene 6*

(*Same scene, without garlic. NATURAL is still lying, now tied up. SARAH, STEVE, and JAX sit on the bench.*)

STEVE: Jax, your mother has something very important to tell you.

SARAH: Jax, (*sighs*) we haven't always told the truth. Not in the slightest.

JAX: What do you mean?

SARAH: (*hesitantly*) Well, those stories that you made up weren't entirely fake.

JAX: See? I told--

SARAH: But they weren't all true either. You see, werewolves and invisible men and giant ice-cream men don't really exist. But monsters do.

STEVE: *Vampires* do.

SARAH: Yes. Vampires do exist. And your mother just so happens to be one.

JAX: That (*pause*) is so cool! Wait, was that you with the parasol then?

SARAH: No, that was your uncle Greg. I've known about Natural for a long time now, and I wanted to make sure you were safe. Greg got hasty and ruined it for all of us.

STEVE: But, I guess you could also say, he saved us as well. (*Nods to NATURAL*) He wouldn't be in that state if it weren't for his little goof.

JAX: Wait, dad, are you a vampire, too?

STEVE: No, just your mother and her family.

SARAH: It was difficult, at first, letting an outsider into our family. But, we learned to trust him and I guess the rest is history.

JAX: So, am I like, half-vampire then?

SARAH: Vampirism doesn't work that way, sweetie. You'd have burned up from the garlic and Holy Water if you were.

JAX: Can you make me a vampire, mom?

SARAH: Maybe when you're older.

JAX: But, what if more vampire hunters attack me?

SARAH: Then I'll come running again, and again, until they stop attacking you. Now, come on. Let's go get some popsicles.

(BLACKOUT)

FIN

# BIOLOGICAL PHENOMENA

There is a biological miracle
That happens when a person opens their mouth to speak.
The air that passes through the vocal chords
Causes them to vibrate,
And sound waves are thus created.
The complete process is quite complex;
However, the result is much simpler to understand.

From there, the rhythm and flow of voice takes control.
When the sound waves reach the far end of the room,
The moment it leaves the lips,
It is a powerful thing.
But it does not have power until voiced.

Voice is a mechanism,
A defensive mechanism,
An offensive mechanism.

Voice is the inspiration,
The infiltration
Of an idea.

Voice is the ambience of emotion
The birthplace of logic.

Voice
Has the complexion
Of the most powerful weapon in the world.
Wield it with care,
For the bullet, when it shoots out of the gun,
Has the power to pass through the hearts and minds
Of everyone.

Voice
Is the gift we are given at birth
To do what we want to do in this world.
Take it, and
Speak.

*Jennifer Chau*

15

# VINTAGE HEART

My love for you is faded
It leaves behind a faint after-taste
Soft and sweet
Like the touch of a forgotten dream
As delicate as butterfly wings and baby eyelashes
As fleeting as a feathered bird and drying hair
I only remember
The glimpses of moments:
The lull of your voice
Your teasing smile and mysterious eyes
Oh—they were no mystery to me, though
It's like we were a part of a fairytale
Somewhere faraway,
Living in an untouchable era of fantasy and joy
I look back at those times
Like how one admires the fading of old photographs
Colors once vivid are worn,
The ink smearing the edges of bodies, hands, and smiles into soft shadows
Holding together memories in blurs
To represent a time that has long-since past
We were so beautiful
And I catch myself almost missing you again.

*Jenny Nguyen*

# THE BROKEN SMILE

The broken smile
is the one that seemed
to stretch for miles.

The disappearing light
is the one that fought
with all of its might.

The torn dream,
is the one that suffered
and lost its gleam.

The hushed voice
is the one that had
to lose its choice.

The beaten heart
is the one who expressed
a tarnished piece of art.

The dulled eye
is the one that watched
as everything waved goodbye.

*Tuyet Duong*

# A LIGHT IN THE DARK

I see a light within the dark.
It glows until I go near.
When I return to bed,
It goes off again.
My night was like this the entire time.
Getting up and down
Turning off the light
Only for it to turn back on.

It annoys me.
I cannot sleep.
That light at 2AM
Continues to keep me up.
Is this my personal hell?
Having to turn the light off
Only for it to turn back on.

Who texts at 2 AM anyways?


*Richard Trejo*

# HE SAT

He sat crossed-legged on my desk,
when I walked into the room
he looked so stressed.
"Listen to me," he said, "Listen."
I'm listening, I promise.

He sat down on my desk.
"Listen to me, please," he said,
"I just need to get something off my chest."
I'm listening, I promise

His voice was shy and timid
but soon his image drifted.
"Listen to me," he said,
"I've been shy my whole life,
but I know with my gut, I want you to be my wife."
I'm listening.

He sat crossed-legged on my desk.
When I walked into the room,
his smile was brighter than ever.
I'm listening, I promise.

*Ashley Rivera*

# EFFLORESCENCE

It's Spring,

and the lovers are in bloom.

See their rosy cheeks and entangled fingers

hear their sighs, their laughter, their whispers.

The air is thick with the sweet scent of love

and they're creating new worlds

between their lips.

*Jenny Nguyen*

# THE UNKNOWN WORLD
## Thaomi Pham

THE SUN DESCENDED BEHIND the mounds and peaks of green hills. The bright orange-yellow pinkish sky transformed into a clear blue. Through the kitchen window, birds sang their usual lovely tune. Like any other Monday, everyone was either at work or in school. The house remained quiet and laid undisturbed, except for tiny noises almost imperceptible to the human ear.

Under the refrigerator, resembling tiny dust balls, were the Kikikumonoes. One was light pink with two antennae. The other, bright teal with no antennae. Though the Kikikumonoes existed in different shapes and color, they all had the same mission: fulfill their hunger, build homes for their families, and avoid human contact.

But then there was Tommy, whom every Kikikumono knew.

"Now be a good boy." Tommy's dad patted and rubbed his son's furry, soft, yellow head.

His dad scurried halfway between the wall and the outer edge then turned around to tell his son, "Remember, don't leave the house unless I tell you to."

Tommy's dad rejoined his armed forces to gather food and materials for the family outside the safety of the refrigerator.

Tommy nodded and waved his antennae. "Yes, Dad."

He waited until they had traveled at least three feet from the fridge. Tommy looked sideways to make sure he could safely step outside.

"Whew. Coast's clear." He fluffy body ran across against the dusty, littered, broken tiles. He was almost to the edge. Jolly Rancher candy wrappers, half-eaten M&Ms, and crushed cheese Cheetos blocked his way, slowing him down. With an inch away from the exit door, Tommy felt a tug.

"Tommy, where do you think you're going?" his mother, a violet Kikikumono with one antenna, asked.

"N-n-nothing, Mom." Tommy's fur rose, frightened.

"Tommy, stop lying to me." She scrunched up her nose and crossed her purple arms. "Haven't your father and I warned you enough? Why don't you ever listen?

21

One day, you'll get yourself injured from the humans of the outside world. By then, it'll be too late. Why can't you--"

"Mom, stop being so overprotective. I'm mature enough to look after myself. I mean what's the worst that can happen to me? I've spent my whole life under this dark, dull, old, unsanitary home. All I want is to explore the outside world and have fun. What's wrong with discovering human culture?"

A crowd of Kikikumonoes snooped behind the walls to observe the argument.

"Tommy." His mother sniffled. "I know that you desire the outside world, but you should think about us Kikikumonoes. If you ventured out of the fridge and a human saw you, all us here would suffocate and perish from poisonous gases. Do you understand that your actions today could've killed us all?"

Uncle John gasped.

"My goodness Tommy," Lily, his oldest sister, shouted.

"I can't believe he even attempted to sneak out of the fridge," Cousin Joe added.

"But mother, I--" Tommy grabbed his head in frustration.

Tommy's aunt came in between him and his mother. "Enough, Tommy."

"But I just--"

His aunt glared at him. "I said enough is enough." She pointed to his room. "Now, go back to your room, Mister."

"Fine." He stomped and headed to his room.

That night, Tommy's mother called him back out of his room to discuss important matters. She beckoned him to sit next to her on the bed made of white and pink erasers.

"Come here, child." She hugged him. "Look, Tommy I'm sorry for lecturing you in front of your aunts, uncles, cousins, and friends. But what you did earlier was absolutely dangerous. As your mother, I want you to be safe."

"Mom... I'm sorry. I didn't know my actions could endanger us all." Tommy kissed his mother on the cheek. "I'm really sorry, Mom. Oh, Mom, about what you said earlier about humans spraying us with deadly and lethal chemicals. What do you mean?"

"Well, the gas was sprayed when I was only three months old. I had been lying in bed while my parents in the other room were chatting away with their guests. The ground shook. Boom. Boom. The sounds of footsteps came nearer and nearer. Our eraser beds and scraps bounced up and down. The brand new tiles cracked and shattered. Some Kikikumonoes screamed in their homes, "It's the end of the world," but the majority of us stood petrified, our antennae trembling. Giant shoes, about thirty feet long and fifteen feet wide in diameter, scraped against our homes. Fumes with a repulsive stench gradually invaded our shelters, choking and suffocating us Kikikumonoes. Fortunately, a few were able to resist the poisonous gas."

"That sounds horrible mom." Tommy's yellow complexion turned a pale daffodil.

"Yes, the tragic event still haunts me today." Tommy's mom shuddered. "Because of this event, the Kikikumonoes enforced strict laws and regulations to protect and ensure safety for all our citizens. Social interactions of any kind with a human result in the death penalty."

"Okay, I understand Mom. I will never communicate with a human ever again," promised Tommy.

However, as the weeks went by, Tommy still pondered about the human world. "Why would humans suffocate us Kikikumonoes?" he asked himself. He climbed and lay down on the blue eraser. One part of him yearned for adventure; the other wanted to avoid the death penalty.

After eight months of avoiding the death penalty, Tommy met with his father.

"Son, since you've turned a little older and become more mature, you should come out with me to hunt food. We should also pick up some scraps along the way to build another room since our family members are increasing."

"Okay, Dad," Tommy said, "I will tag along."

Once he took his step out from the refrigerator, he covered his eyes from the white, intense light. After his eyes adjusted, he looked around. His jaw dropped.

"Wow." Tommy turned his head to observe his surroundings. Stoves, pots, pans, sink, and the microwave amazed him. He jumped with joy and dashed around the human kitchen.

"This human world is heaven." He wandered around, straying from the group. Facing the kitchen table, Tommy remained oblivious to the cat that purred and inched toward his yellow antennae. With her serrated claws, the cat scratched Tommy on the back.

Tommy screamed and ran for his life.

His dad had been rummaging through the trash for food and materials.

"Aaaahh. Someone. Help!" Tommy screamed even louder.

His vision and focus blurred by the pain, Tommy ran straight into Mimi's--a human's--foot. Panicking, Tommy bit her toe. Mimi held her toe and hopped on one leg. "Mom. Something bit me." She wailed.

"I'm sorry, and I didn't mean to hurt you. Please don't cry and please save me from this beast of yours." Tommy grimaced from the pain.

Mimi's mother sprinted towards Mimi and calmed Mimi down." It's okay, sweetheart. It's okay. Mommy's here," Mimi's mother said with a soothing voice. Her mom applied Neosporin on her toe and then bandaged it.

"Someone, please help me," Tommy continually ran away from the cat, running out of air and energy.

Mimi was about to walk away toward her bedroom, until she saw her cat.

"Hello, little Kiwi. I miss you." Mimi gestured the cat toward her. The cat glared at Tommy, but turned its head and ran toward Mimi. "Who's a good little cat?" Mimi petted and hugged her cat.

"Huh ha huh ha." Tommy gasped for air. "Good cat? As if."

Mimi carried her cat into her room, and later went outside to eat dinner. When she gathered the dishes from the cupboard, she spotted Tommy. "What are you doing here, you little puffy guy?" Mimi poked Tommy. "You're so adorable."

"I am a Kikikumono," Tommy replied.

Mimi's eyebrows arched upward, her eyes widening. "Did I hear something? I swear animals can't talk. I'm probably just imagining things. Or is there something wrong with my ears? I should tell my mom." She paused. "Wait. Maybe it really did talk." Her eyes widened. "Maybe this creature really is talking to me." She shrieked then fainted.

"Are you okay?" Tommy shook her part of her shoulder. "Get up."

Mimi's eyes fluttered then opened wide.

"Well, this is going to be silly of me talking to you, but what is your name?" Mimi asked. "And what did you say you are?"

"My name is Tommy. I'm a Kikikumono. And who are you?"

"Mimi."

"Mimi, thank you for saving me from the cat."

"Oh, you're talking about Kiwi? I was just taking her to my room. She's so cute and cuddly."

"Cute and cuddly? That beast of yours nearly killed me."

"Ha-ha. Yea... she likes to chase and catch things. Sorry about that," said Mimi.

Tommy scratched his head. "You know, Mimi you're so nice and kind, but I just don't understand why humans like you would poison my kind with lethal gases. Sometimes, I wonder if humans even have morals or a conscience."

"Sorry to hear that, Tommy. I don't recall any of my family members spraying any chemicals under the fridge though. Oh, wait." Mimi tried to think. "Maybe it's my uncle who came from Texas. He never does his laundry and would wear his old and stinky socks over and over."

Tommy looked disgusted.

"Tell your family and friends that I'm really sorry. It was just an accident. Mom and dad don't believe in using poison in the house."

"I forgive you," Tommy responded. " I also have other questions to ask you. What's it like to be a human? Like what are some aspirations and dreams you possess? What do you learn in school? How does your government work? How about your culture? I'm really want to know."

"Being human is pretty cool, because you get to learn math, language arts, science, history every single day at school. As you grow older, you could become whatever you want if you qualify. When you have a job, you have money. With money, you can buy anything you need," Mimi explained.

"Except of course, lethal gases."

She smiled. "Except that. What about you and your world?"

"In the Kikikumonoes' world, boys have to go with their fathers to find food and build dens for their families when they get older. Girls have to stay home with their mothers and to take care of siblings and cousins. In the Kikikumonoes' world, there are no jobs, money, or schools."

In the distance, Tommy saw a little puffball in the corner of his eye. His first instinct was to go back as fast as he could before he got into any more trouble. "I have to go now, I don't want to worry my father," Tommy said .

"Bye, Tommy."

When Tommy went back to look for his father and the other Kikikumonoes, they were all gone. He went back under the refrigerator. He was welcomed by a crowd of glaring Kikikumonoes. In the back of the crowd, his mother stood crying and moaning about what a terrible son he is.

"Tommy, why? What happened to our promise? I've warned you. It's too late now," Tommy's mother said, sniffling.

Tommy kept silent. Every Kikikumono either ignored or glared at him, including his own dear father.

The Kikikumonoes brought out the rope and strapped Tommy to a pencil, preparing to unleash the vicious, hungry beast called the spider from the box of doom.

Mimi went back to finishing her dinner and thought she heard a little cry echoing from under the fridge. She shrugged and continued to munch on her fried chicken.

Before the death penalty, Tommy uttered, "God save me." The officials lifted the crate and freed the venomous spider. Tommy closed his eyes and accepted his fate.

A pause. At that moment, he felt a gush of air and a splatter of black muck. He opened his eyes to find Mimi and her parents lifting him up, saving him from the death penalty.

"Mimi, how did you-how did you know?" asked Tommy.

"I heard a cry from under the refrigerator, and I wanted to check up on you to see if you were okay," reasoned Mimi.

Tommy scurried toward Mimi. "Thank you. Thank you. Thank you." He burst out with tears of joy. "In my life, I will never find anybody who is as kind and sweet as you."

"Oh, and that reminds me." Mimi squatted down and peered at the others under the refrigerator. " We are sorry to every Kikikumono for the incident that happened years ago. My Uncle Ben didn't mean to spray the chemicals," said Mimi. She kneeled down to grab something. "So, I'm giving this to you and other Kikikumonoes from the bottom of my heart," she revealed a pink doll house.

At first hesitant, Tommy's dad and his hunting team gradually approached the wooden two-story structure. After close inspection, they turned around and nodded approval.

The others cheered. They also went up and down the plastic elevator, played dress up, and hung out with Mimi's dolls.

From that point on, there on after, the Kikikumonoes had a clean and elegant place to live, free of crumbs and dirt, and a peaceful coexistence with the humans, thanks to Mimi.

And thanks to Tommy.

# *ART*

Poetry's always been an art.

The pen is my brush

The paper my canvas

I'm free to write anything that I wish.


A stroke here, a stroke there

A dab and a blop.

I'm going too fast now,

I can't stop.


Only when on my canvas, there is no white

I'll take my brush and sign the bottom right.

And now I have a masterpiece so unique

It could only be created by none other than me.


*Emanuel Ramirez*

# A STRIKING EXPRESSION

Why do we call it love
When a man kisses his wife
        in front of his family,
But beats her
        At home
for not preparing his dinner?

Is it love
When a man spends nights out at the club,
Dancing crazily with another woman,
Touches her
        the way he touches his wife,
But returns home
        with a kiss
                And one dozen roses?

What if, in that bouquet of roses,
Were his secrets and lies,
Embellished with the scent of false love?

Like a rose scented perfume,
He could love,
but only so much
Before the false scent wears away,
Leaving only the odor of lies.

A striking expression,
Such as an "I love you,"
Tainted with lies and abuse and infidelity,
Whatever it may be,
As long as it is coupled with a dozen roses,
Naturally or artificially scented,
Is enough of a charade
For a false sense of satisfaction.

Or even
        a striking gesture,
Like a kiss on the cheek,
With eyes o p e n
        or closed,
After all, hers will be closed,
Is enough to paint a facade
Of a perfect and loving relationship.

As long as a man kisses his wife at the end of the day,
It seems
        To everyone
            That everything
                Is perfectly
   fine.

*Jennifer Chau*

# THE BLUE FLORAL DOOR

I stand in front of her pastel blue door
Reminiscing of when times
used to be simpler

My fingertips slowly tracing
the delicate floral design
My hand lightly gripping
the cold metal knob

I still remember her little hands
Grasping so tightly onto mine
Those were the golden days
The days where she still relied on me
But now she is gone

I can still hear
Her little feet pitter patter
Against the cold wooden floor
Her arms outstretched
for a long awaited hug

My little miracle grew up right before my eyes
One day she brought a little boy over
For a play date
Who knew that one playdate
Would one day turn into a real date

Thinking back to the day where

Little Jimmy came over

To our house and

Sat down on our oversized leather couch

That was the day

that he took her away from me

He asked for her hand


now as time passes

Her fingers are covered with promise rings

Promises of a future he can provide for her

A future only he can provide

Her door still

Remains unopened

The memories of her still linger

I wonder if she'll feel the same

When her little miracle was grows up.


*Nancy Le & Aislinn Stolze*

# SLEEPLESS NIGHTS

Oh boy, I'm up again.
It's 3 AM, I lay there motionless.
The streets are empty
I'm alone with my thoughts.
I don't know how to feel.

I sigh with a heavy heart.
I feel so empty and yet
my mind is filled.
My thoughts are thrilled.
They run and skip and swim.

All these thoughts, these ideas,
they hurt me sometimes.
They're what keeps me up at night.
I try with all my might
to actually get some sleep tonight

But the sun is up now.
There goes another sleepless night.

*Becky Lee*

# UNDESERVED

What is earned?
If you work hard,
for many years,
Then do you deserve it?
That answer up to the asker.
But if you are given a title,
as a "passing of the baton,"
Did you earn it?

That "passing" is a test:
A test of character,
A test of selfishness,
A test of morality.
Will you succumb to greed,
Or stand strong against falsehood?

In this situation,
There are only two sides:
Truth or Lie,
Corruption or Character,
Earned or Given.
You cannot choose a third side.

In my own case,
I was given something
I hated every second of it.
Did I deserve it?
Yes.
Did I earn it?

No.

*Richard Trejo*

# BEEP-BEEP-BEEP
Kari Nguyen

I DON'T KNOW WHAT happened. I was in a car, going to my grandma's for her birthday. Then, the noises. The banging, the screeching, the screaming. Then nothing. Pitch-black nothing.

*Where am I? Am I awake? Why can't my eyes open? My body feels stiff and I can't move. Why can't I move? All I hear is the beep beep, beep beep next to me, and all I feel is the fluffy blanket on top of me. But why am I so cold?*

It's been a couple of weeks since I've been here. People come in and poke me every now and then. I always ask them, "Hey, can someone tell me what's happened to my eyes? I can't open them," but get no response.

I think those people who poke me know what they are doing. They poke me in the same place every time, sometimes with their finger, and sometimes with something sharp. I don't know what it is, but it hurts. I want to swat at them, tell them to stop and tell them to help me, but I can't do anything else but lie there and take the pain. These people don't talk much. They just poke, sigh, and leave.

A warm hand glides over and grasps my hand every now and then, and it's always accompanied by stories. She is on the seventh chapter of <u>Harry Potter and the Order of the Phoenix</u> now. I want to tell her, *"I've already read it."* I can't. Other times, she just sits next to me, holding my hand in silence with the beep-beep-beep in the background.

She cried today. Her tears fell on my hands, and her sniffling was muffled into her shirt. She must have noticed that she got me dirty, because she scrubbed my hands with her shirt. I wanted to cheer her up, but I couldn't hug her. I couldn't even raise my arms an inch. Some people came into the room while she was crying and said, "You should leave the room" and "You shouldn't be here for this." I didn't recognize the voices.

*Something is wrong, definitely wrong. I don't want my mom to go. I am so scared.* She cries louder and yells, "No, he's still here. My boy is still here."

I want to shout, "Of course I'm still here. Where else would I be?" I hear some grunting, then everything becomes quiet.

Mom comes back later, sniffling. She sits down and cries, louder and louder, until she is almost screaming. Then she hits me across the face. I feel the place where she slapped me burn. I don't know what I did wrong, but she keeps hitting me. Again and again and again. I can't stop her or cry or say sorry. I can only lay there until two men come in and take her away.

They yell at her, "There is nothing else we can do. We have to let him go."

*What is going on?*

Two other men come in and mumble some things that I can't make out anything they say until I catch something. "Coma."

I finally understand. I want to scream, to shake, to jump up and down, and slap him across the mouth. But I can't. I can't say, "Please, I'm here. I can hear you. Please don't do this to me." Nothing. I just lie there, as they poke me with the needle. The beep-beep-beeps turns into beep-beeps. *I'm getting tired.*

I scream at the top of my lungs and thrash my arms, but I'm not moving.

*I don't want them to inject me with anything. I don't want the beep-beep-beeps to go away. I don't want to die. I need to tell my mom that everything is going to be okay, tell her that I'm here and that I'm fine. I want to tell her that I love her.* But I guess I can't do that anymore.

Beep.

Beep.

—

# LOVELY LITTLE LADY

Tell me, from the start
Is it possible
To fall for art?

You know, George?
Oh don't you?
After shaping little lady
And falling for her too

The slender long arms
With slim dancer's legs
She was a lovely clay lady
Made with color of nutmeg

She couldn't talk
But oh was she beautiful
She had a little laugh
That was oh so musical

She listened to George's woes
Lay by him for the night
Only the next morning
She was nowhere in sight

And George realized
as he looked at the mound
Why she had disappeared
And didn't make a sound

The moment he made her
With every delicate curve
He forgot the crucial step--
to paint her with preserve

*Alexandra Quang*

# *YOU*

My arms are the ones

That hold you at 3 o'clock in the morning.

When you're crying, wondering if you should stay.

You should stay.

I love you.

My voice is the one that silences

The voices inside your head.

The ones that haunt you.

The ones that scare you.

I'm here, don't be scared.

I love you.

My eyes are the ones

That see the beauty in your existence .

When your eyes can't.

You're beautiful.

I love you.

My heart is the one

That gives you all it has to give

Tries to give you the will to live

Because

I love you.

*Kimberly Viramontes*

# KEEP SEARCHING

I've spent ages looking for it.

Looking for that feeling.

I am still unclear where to look.

Do I look for it in people?

Or in materialism?

Why is it so hard to find?


There was one point

when I was sure I found it.

That feeling

of being whole.

I felt complete.

I felt happy.

Unfortunately,

he did not.


Hopeless and scared,

I force myself to search.

I know why it's so hard to find.

It's not in others,

It's in me.

I'm just too afraid

To grow up.


*Noah Sabatini*

# DROWNING

I touch the water with my toe.
Cold, like it always is.

I look back to my parents.
"We love you."
"I love you too."
We both lie and wave goodbye with hands we once held together.

I go to bed, my parents there with genuine smiles I can't feel.
"Good night. We love you."
"I love you too."
We both lie, as I lie in bed watching them leave the room.

I wake up screaming about the
nightmares that haunt me since then.
"You're safe here."
And yet I only feel the cool water surrounding me once again.

*Nicole Le*

# EVERYTHING FOR A GLIMPSE

The dedication is something
that I have not seen before.
Everything they do,
every action they take,
it is all for a glimpse.

They spend money, like water,
to support those they love.
Just to get closer to them.
Just to see them amongst the crowd
because they can do nothing more
than steal a glimpse.

They travel miles,
fly across oceans,
rent hotels in unfamiliar places
so they can be near the ones they love,
watch them for minutes, even mere seconds
to capture a glimpse.

Everything they see,
captured in their lens,
snapped by cameras
hanging around their necks.
They spend hours, give up nights
editing the photos they have
to assure that other people
can have a glimpse, too.

*Christina Nguyen*

# *REALITY*

Cinderella:

As a child, I thought I was that princess

As a teenager, I realized that's childish

But the beauty of being a child is not knowing your limits

and believing you can do all of it.


As you grow,

You'll learn then know

That those big dreams and millions of aspirations

are not all attainable.

You learn about time, requirements, and qualifications

Once you learn, you realize;

Realize that you are simply human with limitations


*Gina Nguyen*

# CLANWOOD
## Hellen Pham


HADLEY HAD HEARD ABOUT this hideous creature in stories. The one with yellow, wrinkly, skin, thin body, and oval head. It could travel fast and float in mid-air without legs. Its gaping hole for a mouth sucked in souls like a vacuum, and its screams were deafening and bloodcurdling.

Hadley's older brother used to teased her and give her nightmares that lasted for weeks, but never in her adult life did she believe it were real. She had almost completely removed it from her memories, but it had returned, and now, it was haunting her.

The horrid creature caught her scent with its snake-like nose. Its slits flared.

"Run! Hadley, run!" was the last thing she heard her brother scream as the creature caught up to him. It ripped out his soul and ate his heart, for it had neither. Although it didn't have eyes, Hadley felt it glaring at her, targeting her as prey.

Hadley sprinted past the trees in the woods. It was dark, and she nearly tripped. Only slivers of moonlight through crowded branches lighted her path.

She remembered how guilty her brother felt for scaring her. He gave her a necklace with a jagged piece of silver for safety and comfort. He said it was holy and would protect her from any monster. *He promised,* but she never believed it would work.

Now, it was her turn to hunt the gruesome thing. She had to be the bait, the trap. She heard the crunching of bones. Blood dripped from its lipless smile and crooked, pointy teeth. It shrieked. Hadley prepared her necklace and fashioned it onto a leash. "Come and get me."

It challenged her. *It's not afraid,* Hadley thought. *Why is it not afraid? Doesn't it sense the silver?* Hadley charged, and it scratched at her. Her arms and face were cut, but she thought she had managed to chain it.

It's boney, witchy claws broke her necklace.

"It didn't work," Hadley cried.

Once again in this game of cat and mouse, Hadley became the prey. She cowered on the ground, ready to face the same fate and join her brother. She was prepared to meet her end, wherever it was.

Instead, the monster stretched out its rough, patchy hand to help her up.

Hadley lay on the ground, stunned and confused. *Why... why isn't it killing me? Why is it helping me?*

Unbeknownst to her, when she chained the monster, Hadley had created a bond between the two. It took no leash; the monster had destroyed it, but she had tamed it. It was ready to follow, to serve, but Hadley wasn't convinced. "I hate you," she cried. "You killed my brother. I will never keep you as a pet."

Hadley pounced on the monster and took it in her grip, choking the life out of it. Her hand reached for her survival knife and almost ended its life when a figure of a tall middle-aged man approached them. With powerful hands, the man grabbed Hadley's shoulder and pried her off the monster.

"Look at me," he said. Hadley turned to him, her face still intent and furious. "Killing it won't bring your brother back. It only makes you as evil as it is."

Hadley backed away and let the man take control. He cuffed the creature and dragged it over to his black SUV, waiting nearby. By the time he came returned, the sun was rising. Everything felt gray.

"Thank you." Hadley looked up at him, her arms bruised and bloodied, her hair matted with dirt and sweat.

"Oh, don't thank me," he said. "You had a wrangle on that monster all by yourself."

"How long were you watching?"

"I--"

"You knew it killed my brother," Hadley said. Her hands clenched into fists. "You didn't think to step in at any point? Who are you, and why weren't you there to save us? To protect us?"

"I'll explain," he said. "I am Agent Brian Callahan. I work for S.O.B."

"Son of a--?"

"No. Supernatural Order Bureau. It's an underground society. The world you call California, we call Clanwood. My orders are to rescue 'monsters.' I couldn't let you kill it. The bureau hides and shelters them from the 'normal' society. Again, I am sorry for the loss of your brother. And wow--"

"Wow?"

"I'm surprised you're taking everything so well."

"Don't get me wrong. I'm not." She looked up at him. "What am I supposed to do?"

"Do you believe what I'm telling you?"

"Of course I believe you. I saw it with my own eyes. They're real."

"As real as you and me. And just like people, some are bad eggs." He pointed to the creature.

"Callahan, can I tell you something? When I was younger, I've always felt like I had a hidden sixth sense that mythical creatures were real. I just wasn't expecting this."

"Me neither. As a kid, I had so many imaginary friends. My parents always thought I would grow up to be something creative. I'm a cop now."

"I saw them as a kid, and the thing is, Callahan, it just never stopped."

"What about your brother? Did he have the Sight?"

"He did. Now, he's dead. I prefer if you don't mention him right now."

"I understand," Callahan said.

"I'm sorry, it's just… he helped me get my Sight. He confirmed everything I saw. We believed in the good beings even when our parents tried to drill us to stop. I thought this one was made up. He had always warned me about it. Isn't that ironic?"

Callahan only nodded.

"How am I going to explain this to my family?"

"This being hunts the same season mountain lions do. It's smart and hides its tracks that way."

"A mountain lion mauled my brother," Hadley said, scoffing.

"Your brother is a hero. He sacrificed himself so you could get away. He seems like a great man."

Hadley smiled, eyes watering.

"He is. You would've liked him. Everyone likes him." She turned to Callahan and wiped her tears. "I never did introduce myself before I barked at you, did I? My name is Hadley."

"Nice to meet you." Callahan smiled and shook her hand. "Hadley, I know this seems heartless after your experience, but I'm going to need to take you into my station so we can fill out a report. You can take all the time you need. Then, you can reunite with your family. I'll help explain it to them."

"Hadley, I need to tell you the truth. There's another reason I've brought you here, and it's because I've been looking for new recruits for S.O.B."

"You want me?"

"You've maintained this gift ever since you were a child. You never truly stopped believing, and your brother helped you develop a powerful vision."

"And it killed him and nearly got me killed, too. I don't exactly have a great first-hand experience with this job."

"You're one of the few special people, Hadley."

"So? And 'special'? I should've been dead! My brother should be here filling the papers for me. I was his responsibility. He was older and always had to protect me, and now, he died for me. It's not fair."

"I wanted you to come with me not only to fill the report, but to experience this. And to not let the legacy he made go to waste. I'm sure he would've wanted this, too."

Hadley was skeptical, but Callahan knew how to deal his cards.

"Fine," she said, grabbing the lapels of his coat, "but next time, don't guilt trip me using my brother, okay?"

"Yes ma'am. Thank you so much, Hadley. You won't regret this."

"I already have."

# A STAIRCASE TO HEAVEN

Where the moon rises,

so does the sun.

The higher you climb the vivid staircase

the sooner you find yourself there:

the place where hopes and faith transpire.

Let the people dance and flutter in the endless boundaries

Let the soft colors of the wind lift you from your feet

Touch the clouds that gently comfort you

Dance with the random shapes in the sky

Raise the flags of this new realization

The realization that you're in heaven.

*Maggie Tieu*

# THE LONELY WALK

If I told you that a flower bloomed in a dark room, would you believe me?
Would you say I love you back if I told you that
I love you?
Yes,
They are white lies.
White lies that I chose to believe
because I'm in the mood for your empathy.
I wish you truly did love me
so I could show you what love really is.

What kind of man
treats you so wrong, for so long -
yet you still love him.
I ask you about those purple bruises,
but you change the subject

I see you in a corner
just trying to put yourself together.
Looking through your thoughts
and looking over your shoulders.
Asking why he comes home and beats you
until there are blood stains all over your favorite carpet
I see you crying in the corner.
Thinking that it was your fault
but it wasn't.

Mom,
he doesn't love you like I do.
Let me show you what love really is

Overtime you became absorbed, oblivious to the time
that he says that he loves you,
cares for you,
wouldn't hurt you again.
He says to you that he will change
He will become a better man than before.
When?
When will that happen, mother?
Ask yourself how many times he has told you,
has shown you multiple times with those dark purple bruises,
those holes in the walls that he has thrown you into
that you try to cover up with something beautiful
And that scar, that scar you have in your heart.

So ask yourself: does he really love you?
It's time for you to leave,
To leave this horrendous love that you're in

Am I the flower?
The flower that blooms beautifully in the dark room
No, I am not
You are the beautiful flower that blooms in the dark room
You may look good on the outside
but the flower is full of bees but no honey

The flower that is blossoming from a broken home
The flower that searches out for sunlight
Like you search out for someone's love for you
Your petals have bright colors
Bright colors that are your personality
But each time you pluck your petals
For people that you want to give,
so you can receive back a petal
But only receive thorns that cut through your stem
From a broken home, you weren't taught what love looked like
Or what the meaning of love was
So let me show you what it is
Just grab my hand and I'll teach you the meaning of true love

It may seem that I'm not there for you but
I am
I will be there for you when you get lost
in the hopeless path you are in
I will be there for you when you need a shoulder to cry on
I will be there for you when you need someone's love
Never forget me
Like I have never forgotten you

You are not alone in that lonely path
It doesn't have to be a long lonely walk from home
You ask me what is home
Home that you haven't really had
Home that you haven't felt
Home that has love
But together we can make a home
That is filled with beautiful flowers that will grow
with each other having an unbreakable power
called love.

*Stephanie Vivar*

47

# I ASSURE YOU!

I assure you,

Your future is completely safe!

No harm, or worries needed

Your case has already been pleaded

That you should go out there and do whatever you want

Be it a doctor, a teacher-moonlighting-actor,

Realtor, or someone that browses live on Twitch through a browser, type TOR.

I assure you,

Your future is completely safe!

Just consign yourself to ten-thousand hours of practice,

And all you have to do is pass that class and this

It's so easy!

Sign your SSN to that sleazy scholarship offer

And watch your credits rack up in someone else's coffer

And I assure someone will be right there at the counter,

Ready with all ⅛ of the instructions

As to how you're going to be eligible in a jiffy

For that class and this; probability : very iffy

And "Too bad, this deadline you missed right there

Has evaporated all your registration progress into thin air!"

And I assure you, that AP Physics class won't count

Only in mind you'd know more than the average person taking hundreds out of

their account

Who paid his or her way through discounts

But I can assure you, sir or ma'am

Or whatever this gender-paletted generation would like to call itself

You're helping yourself if you apply to this fraternity

I'll be frank with you, this'll only put star athletes into the annals for eternity.

I assure you,

Don't turn your head away from this prestigious university!

They're not milking your loans for the sake of perfidy;

They just want to capitalize on your triumphs over all this adversity!

For this limited, highly-contested offer of a quarter-million loan

We'll make your mind so strong, so grown

That you'll own a throne worth millions…

…once you dedicate over five more years to shadowing and fellowships.

I'll admit this part of life is the far nastier bit

BUT!

I assure you,

If you follow this tediously teetering way

You'll have your payday

And your future might just be, one day,

Completely safe.

*Vincent Nguyen*

# RIGHT BEFORE ME

I gaze up at the starry
sky at night.
Every speck of light glistens
before my eyes.
The universe right before me.

I reach up and collect
stars, preserving them in
mason jars.
Categorizing them by size
every piece of the
universe is my wish.

My wish to conquer the galaxy,
formed by deep explosions,
and galactic collisions.

As the universe expands,
we discover planets,
but as we discover more,
the lonelier the universe
becomes.

Gradually my stars begin
to fade,
as well as the universe.

"Before I vanish, I must
Rearrange the constellations
Into fallen heroes and objects."

Connect the dots of each
constellation to
discover a story of their own.

Hidden meanings,
loose interpretations.

My gaze dwindles,
my eyes brighten
one last time.

A galactic movement
pleases my eyes.
Icy asteroids fall,
a meteor shower begins,
and exploding supernovas.

My body stops at such a
sight. Unable to continue
Or move.

As the stars finally crash,
I know the end has greeted
me, foreshadowing my descent.

I gaze up at the once starry sky
one last time.
Every speck of light is now
black and white.
And the universe before me
has never been so bright.

*Allison Tran*

# THE TOWN WHERE STARS FALL

The Town Where Stars Fall

Speckles that glisten across the land, glimmering through the dark night

Below the moon, below the galaxy, below the heavens is where they lie

The hopes that it carries is what makes it shine bright

But within those boundaries lies another name

The town where stars fall, illuminating the darkness

Filling in the cracks of ambition and passion

It becomes the concrete that lays the foundation for dreams

Expanding, Bustling, Rumbling, the streets are always filled

Musicians, Actors, Writers flock, bringing with them a sense of determination

Wanting to shine and leave their own mark

So that one day they too can be a star and be luminous

They too want to be a part of the town where stars fall

*Kevin Ho*

# SO, SO BEAUTIFUL

Isn't it so beautiful
The way the sun peaks
From behind the
Silhouette of the hills

And isn't it beautiful
How the clouds drift
So far
Just to see the world

And the wind
and flowers
and trees
And stars
Aren't they so beautiful

And what would happen
If they were taken away from you
Ripped out of your powerless hands
Then what would happen if they
Covered your eyes with the delusions and
The memories

And how would you feel if
You sit in a world of darkness
Emptiness
Nothing

So, so beautiful

*Kari Nguyen*

# *JON*
## Zachary King

JON STOOD ON THE table and shouted to the crowd, "Who wants to see a backflip?"

The crowd, nearly the entire population of Bardsdale, erupted in laughter. "Do it, John. Don't leave us waiting," they shouted back.

The tavern was particularly bright this evening, and the normal sounds of the band and people's voices were drowned out by the group surrounding the dwarfish man standing on the table. Men who were normally passed out at this time of night were wide awake, waiting for their new townsman to face plant, head-first into the wooden floorboards.

Jon crouched down and leaned forward, splitting his green trousers. He sprung back and landed flat on his face. "I got hurt," he cried.

A week ago, Jon had wandered into town looking for a place to stay with nothing but the clothes on his back and a giant, blue rock. He said he was from "over there," but he pointed in a different direction every time he said so. He said he was staying with his "Unkie Joseph," who went missing a day before Jon's arrival. They let him stay in his Uncle Joseph's cottage anyway. Every morning, he wandered down the paved roads, greeting every stone on the ground. He would reach the market and grab the biggest, juiciest fruit he could find and stuff it down his gullet right then and there. The townspeople put it on a tab for when Joseph returned or when the news of his death arrived, whichever happened first. Jon would then go home, say goodbye to all the stones, and shut himself in for the rest of the night.

This week was different. The townspeople, one by one, invited Jon to spend the night at the tavern with them, and, after receiving an invitation from nearly every person in Bardsdale, he agreed. After a few drinks, he nearly cracked his skull on the tavern floor after attempting a sideways backflip, making it one of the dumbest stunts anyone had seen since his arrival.

Two men grabbed Jon by the wrists and pulled him up while a man in battered steel armor flung open the door. A hush fell over the bar. The man pulled off his helmet, letting his long, brown hair flow down as he strutted in the building. The ladies, faces red as tomatoes, sighed and giggled to themselves as he walked by.

"I'll have a pint, miss," he said, leaning against the counter. On the house, I expect?"

The waitress smiled. "Anything for you, Mikael."

"Mikael," shouted a man from across the bar, "Come over here and tell us about your latest quest."

He frowned as he approached a crowd of middle aged men. The scent of beer and cigarettes greeted his nostrils.. "You think sailing for weeks out in sea is fun? I plundered ship after ship only to find that their flags were forgeries. I left my people for months, and after all this torture, all this pain, all this misery, what do I get? I'll tell you what I got. A gem." He slammed a dime-sized onyx gemstone on the table. "A measly little artifact that has only monetary value. Do you know how many men I lost on that ship, how much blood I have stained on my hands just for this little ... this thing?"

"I didn't realize how much it affected you, Mikael," one man said, nearly whispering, his head hung in shame.

"It doesn't," he said, sipping his ale. "You should've seen your faces though. I really had you going there, didn't I?"

"I'm Jon," a voice said from behind.

Mikael turned to face the man. After tripping over floorboards broken by Jon's antics, Mikael spilled his drink.

"Jon?" Mikael asked. "I don't remember any Jon coming around here before."

"He just got here last week," a man said. "Joseph's nephew. His uncle high-tailed it outta here, though. Probably not comin' back."

Mikael scanned the man standing before him: green overalls, beer belly, and bruised face. He extended his hand, the other still rubbing the bump on his head.

"Pleased to meet you, Jon. I'm Mikael. Warrior. Adventurer. Lover." He shot a wink to the wench behind the bar.

"Do you wanna be my friend?" Jon asked.

"Well." Mikael stuttered. He whispered to the table, "What's his deal anyway?"

"He's not right in the head, Mick," one whispered back. "He swallows the biggest fruit whole every day."

"How does he pay for it?"

The man shrugged his shoulders.

"Well, Jon," Mikael said, "I don't really know you all that well, and you just got here-"

"Okay. I got hurt. Gonna go home now." John said. He turned to leave, still rubbing the lump on his head.

A *boom* stopped him in his tracks. Flames covered the view from the windows as the sounds of a dragon swooping over the village drowned out the screams of the people. The tavern roof caught fire. Outside, a massive black shadow spat fire across the town. It ate half of the town's livestock and people. The men and women in the bar ran outside, screaming for shelter. Some ran for the hills, and some sought shelter. Jon ran for his uncle's cottage. Mikael pulled him away and dragged him towards the rest of the townspeople. They set up camp on a hill a mile away and watched their hometown burn. Moments later, the dragon flew away with a sizeable teal stone in its claws.

"It's retreated," Mikael said. "Did anyone see that rock?"

"That's mine," Jon shouted. He sprinted after the dragon. "Give it back, you monster. Give it back."

Mikael seized Jon by the arm. "What do you mean *yours*?"

"My rock. My shiny rock. It's mine. I want it back."

A man approached the two. "Mikael, that's the second time this month that that dragon's attacked our village. We've sent party after party to hunt it down, but none of them have come back alive. He lives in a canyon, past the golden forest." The man bowed and dropped to one knee. "Will you, great hero, do us the honor of slaying that foul beast?"

Mikael crossed his arms. "It's my duty to protect and serve this village for all it's done for me. Now, it's time to pay my dues," he shouted. He made sure everyone heard him. "In the name of Bardsdale, I shall slay this dragon."

The crowd of men and women shouted and clapped, chanting his name to the heavens. Everyone cheered for his name but Jon, who was still mourning the loss of his shiny stone.

"I'm going, too." Jon stood up and put his hand on Mikael's shoulder.

Mikael laughed. "That's ridiculous. A fool like you? You couldn't harm a legless sheep, let alone a dragon."

Jon stepped forward until he was inches away from Mikael's face.. "I'm going. It's my stone."

Mikael gave an evil grin. "Go for it, Jon. You can come too."

The crowd erupted in gasps and whispers. "Is he crazy? What's wrong with him? Is he stupid too?"

Mikael turned to the crowd and raised his hands. "Jon, go pack your things."

Jon turned around and skipped back to his house.

"Do not think me foolish, people," Mikael said. "I know what I am doing."

"Then tell us, Mick," a man shouted.

"This fool pays for nothing, correct?"

The crowd murmured agreeing words.

"And he's responsible for the broken floorboards in the tavern, correct?"

The crowd murmured louder.

"And according to Jon, that stone belongs to him?"

The crowd simultaneously shouted, "Yeah."

"Then listen to my plan. I cannot kill innocent men. I have done that far too often in my past, but I shall take Jon with me and leave him in the golden woods where he, with his supreme intellect, will have no chance of survival. He will not bother anyone ever again; I shall slay this dragon and eliminate the two beings that plague this village."

The crowd clapped and cheered. Mikael ran back into town, where he and a few men built a makeshift cart, rounded up some slightly-charred horses, and stuffed Jon in the back. The village waved, cheered, shouted, "Good luck," and "Godspeed, Mick," as the pair drove into the woods.

"So, Jon. You realize that this mission will make you a hero, right?"

"I love my stone."

"Yes, Jon, that is what we're going to get."

Jon sang, "Stone, stone, stone, stone, stone, stone, stone, stone."

"Can you not--"

"Don't you like my singing?" Jon asked.

"What have I gotten myself into?" Mikael whispered to himself. "It's not that I don't like it, Jon. I just need to concentrate. Yes, I need to concentrate."

"Okay," Jon said, smiling. He hummed the tune to himself.

Days passed as they wandered through the forest. Every morning, Mikael would hunt for their breakfast, and every afternoon, he would hunt for their supper. Jon spent most of his time having enlightening conversations with the horses, which consisted mainly of neighs rather than actual English.

After two weeks of travelling, the duo reached about halfway into the forest. Mikael stopped the horses in the afternoon sun, which was shaded by yellow trees.

"What happened?" Jon asked.

"I need you to do something for me, Jon. You see, I'm still so hungry, but I need to tend to the horses. Do you think you can go fetch some berries?"

Jon nodded his head. He ran off into the woods as Mikael jumped onto the horses and whipped as hard as he could. Jon turned back around upon hearing the noise and ran after the cart. But he wasn't nearly fast enough. After a few minutes, his breathing got heavy, and he stopped chasing the cart altogether.

Jon trudged through the forest, thinking about how he had made the villagers smile. "I'll show him," he thought, "I'll go back to the village and tell everyone about his little trick. They'll have him killed."

Jon realized that he had no idea where the village was. He was too deep into the forest to see anything but trees, so he picked a direction and walked. He arrived at a cliff side lined with rocks, where he took off his shirt and folded it into a pillow. He then lied down and drifted off to sleep.

"Foolish human, who are you to enter my domain?" a voice called from below.

Jon woke with a start. He peered over the cliff to see Mikael cornered in the canyon below, stared down by the massive, blue dragon that destroyed his village.

"I-I-I am Mikael," he whimpered, "and I've come here to -um- strike a-a deal, oh great dragon, sir."

The dragon huffed a mighty bellow. "I'll give you a deal." He raised his claw. "You leave now, and I might spare your life." He swung his claw down.

"Hi, dragon," Jon called. The dragon turned and stared up at Jon.

"Who are you?" The dragon called.

Mikael shouted from the bottom, "Run, Jon. Save yourself."

A rumbling came from beneath the rocks as Jon turned around. A landslide covered the dragon in stone. Jon tumbled and spun down the hill. Mikael ran to him at the bottom.

"Are you alright, Jon?" He grasped Jon's hand and tried in vain to pull him up.

The pile of rocks shifted and rumbled as Mikael tried desperately to carry Jon and his beer belly. The dragon's head burst out of the pile, scattering rocks and sending them tumbling down the hill.

"You humans are always such pests. Look at you, coming here and taking my most powerful possession, and when I try to get it back, you try to kill me as if it was yours. Such arrogance." The dragon bent down and picked Mikael up in his teeth. "Now, you will suffer for all of your kind." The dragon took in a deep breath, but before he could do anything, a whistle from the canyon interrupted him.

Jon, with one hand against his stone, stood staring the dragon straight in the eye. "Mikael," he shouted, "catch." He picked up the rock in both hands and hurled it at the dragon's head. It fell over onto the pile of rocks. Jon ran back over to the stone and grasped it with both hands.

"Friend, there is only one way to kill this beast," Jon said.

"Jon, you've managed to say more than three words in a sentence-"

"This isn't the time for jokes. I'll explain everything later. For now, I need you to chip away at this rock until you chip off a pointed shard. Use that to kill the beast."

Mikael did as he was told, striking small pieces of rock off with his sword. He worked faster as the dragon shifted under the rocks. The dragon raised its head again, wobbling back and forth. He turned to Mikael once more and picked him up in his mouth. Jon picked up a thin, pointed shard off the ground. "Hey dragon."

"What, human?"

"Hi." Jon threw the crystal spear straight at the dragon's neck, killing it instantly. He picked up the rock again and carried it with him as he and Mikael headed back to the cart. The ride was silent for the first few days.

"Why do you act like such a fool all the time?" Mikael asked, breaking the silence.

"What do you mean?" Jon asked. He polished the rock with his shirt.

"It's very obvious you have quite a bit of intellect. Why not show it?"

"I can't, friend. Not without this stone. That dragon, Bard, put a curse on me the first time I encountered him. He poured all my intelligence into this stone."

"So touching it allows you to regain your intelligence?"

"And letting go removes it. It being a giant stone, I didn't wish to burden myself carrying it around with me throughout town. I've kept it in my uncle's house. That's where I did research and tracked down that dragon to find its weaknesses. I'd hoped that slaying it would lift the curse, but I guess I was wrong."

Jon and Mikael strolled into the newly-rebuilt town. Mikael waved at the cheering people. Jon sat still, with one elbow leaning on the blue rock. The people laughed and sneered as he passed by.

"People, people, if you will," Mikael started. The crowd fell silent. "The dragon is slain. Jon's rock has been recovered." The crowd fell silent.

"Jon, will you explain to these good people what you have told me?"

"Certainly." Jon leaned his body against the stone. "Good people, I am not a moron," he began. Mikael grinned as he scanned the audience's faces.

"... I was dead wrong," Jon said, finishing his speech. He sat down. The crowd was silent. They were shocked.

"You left out one small detail, Jon," Mikael shouted. "Had it not been for Jon's clever wit and cunningness, with or without his rock, I would not be alive. He saved my life, more than once within minutes, and for that, I owe him my sincerest gratitude." He stepped off the cart and bowed to Jon. Slowly, the rest of the crowd joined him. Jon stood, let go of the rock, and stepped off the cart. The crowd gasped.

"Hi, Mikael," he said.

"Hello, Jon," Mikael said. "Hello, hero."

# MY DEFINITION OF PERFECTION

I stand before you
Eyes closed
Hands at my side
And my head held high
Waiting for you to judge me.

Fat? Is my face too round,
Are my thighs too big?
Am I not skinny enough for you?
You want me to be taller?
How? I stopped growing years ago
I'm sorry that I'm not your definition of perfection

I open my eyes and stare
Do I like the person who is staring back ?
This broken, lifeless person
Have I learned to accept myself for who I am?
Or have I lowered my standards
So you'll accept me for being someone I'm not

I stand before myself
I close my eyes
Unclench my hands
Relax my back
And I wait
How do I see myself?

I open my eyes and I stare
Examining every flaw, imperfection, blemish on my body
I look at myself and realize
That I love my the way I look
I love every flaw I have

I look at myself and finally understand
I don't care how you see me
Because it doesn't matter.
I'm not your definition of perfect
But I am my own definition of perfection.

*Mikayla Reilly*

# PENCIL

A pencil,

The most important utensil,

That would encode notes,

That would record history,

That would support imagination,

A masterpiece of creation,

an aid to invention.

I lost my special pencil,

I'm nothing without that pencil,

Not an author, journalist, nor historian.

Without that pencil, I can't do anything.

This object is sentimental.


*Thaomi Pham*

# ODE TO THE MIDNIGHT SOUL

Side by side, we sat
In those exact chairs I see now
Delightful buzz of chatter in my ear
We held hands in the dawn of light
As we sipped the bitter sweetness of eternity.

You and I, that's what you said
Forever and ever is what we sang
Only the moonlit sky now burns bright
Fireflies the only one to sing
I love you, I said
A mere glassy smile in return.

A man now down on one knee
I couldn't help but to wash it all down
A shot of whiskey, if you'd please
The night which once belonged to us
The stars shine bright, my dear
A forgotten love doth ring."

*Tiffany Leiterman*

# FALLEN FANTASY

If one day the sky stopped shedding tears,
If one day the sun just disappears,
If one day the earth starts standing still
And the moon stops rising over the hill…
In the end, I will be there to witness.

If darkness were to consume the world
And the faintest rays of light lie in the smallest
And rarest of endangered deeds of good,
Humanity has already been swallowed,
Bathing too long in the company of demons.

If one day the ocean waves fail to rise,
If one day the air is polluted with demise,
If one day all that I hold dear shatters
And the blood red of roses scatters…
In the end, I will still be there to witness

So now, I hold all that I love close
as tentatively as I would, as I could;
Never letting go, or convince myself so
As I watch the seams of miracles unravel
To be embraced by spite and anger.

If one day I were to breathe my last breath,
If one day I were to be an existence no more,
The whole world would still decline into death
When the world makes little of the good before
And plummet further into this fallen fantasy.

*Yen Tran*

# MERELY A GOLDFISH

A fish with its nose
Against the glass of a small fishbowl,
Looking over the sea,
Dreaming.

What would I do,
What would I be,
If I were just down there,
Swimming,
Free?

Would I be a mermaid,
Or, or a shark?
I would plunge into the abyssal zone,
Mysterious and
Dark.

But alas, alas,
I am bound by glass,
This invisible force-field.
My prisoner fate,
Sealed.

My human captors,
So idle, so vain,
Believe me,
a free-swimming
individual,
To be like them,
The same.

But I am not.
I wish to journey,
To challenge the sea,
And swim and swim,
Unbounded and free,

To the pinnacle of all that
I can be.

But by fate,
I was not meant for
The sea,
Because evolution has rendered me
Merely a goldfish,
Tiny,
Unfree.

*Monica Van*

# SWEET DREAMS

Thong Pham

CHARACTERS:
SIMON: *a middle-aged male therapist*
FRED: *A man in his mid-20's*
POLICE: *Self-explanatory*

Scene 1

*(Noon, present day. In office, with mahogany floorboards and earthly wallpaper. An oaken desk littered with papers sits at one end of the room, under the only window. There is a lofty sofa and velvet chair facing each other, with a coffee table between them. A teapot boils in a corner, and a potted plant stands next to the sofa. SIMON sits in the chair, scribbling on a clipboard.)*

SIMON:     Hmmm…Perhaps…No. That's a horrible idea. *(crosses out something on his notepad)* Wait…that could work. I'll just have to-
FRED:     *(knocks on door)* Hello?
SIMON:     It's open. Come on in.
FRED:     *(enters left)* Um, hello .
SIMON:     Please, have a seat. *(gestures to sofa)*
FRED:     *(flops down on sofa)* Thank you for having me on such short notice Doctor…Fraud?
SIMON:     Freud.
FRED:     *(fidgets)* Freud, yes. Of course. Sorry, Doctor Freud. I'm not myself lately.
SIMON:     Oh, it's no trouble at all, Mr. Darwin. We all have our off days.
FRED:     Off-day is an understatement. I haven't slept all week.
SIMON:     That explains the fidgeting.
FRED:     Oh--sorry, Doctor.
SIMON:     No trouble, Mr. Darwin. No trouble at all. *(scribbles on his notepad)* Perhaps some tea will do you good.
FRED:     Yes. Please. Anything to help me stay awake.
SIMON:     *(walks over to stove and prepares two cups)* Sugar?
FRED:     One lump.
SIMON:     *(hands FRED a cup and sits back down)* Imported from a garden in

Osaka. Do enjoy. (*raises cup*)

FRED:    Thank you, Doctor. You're too kind.

SIMON:    I do my best to help my patients relax. It makes opening up easier.

FRED:    I always enjoy tea. (*takes a sip and spits out the tea, gagging for air*)

SIMON:    Not a fan of Jasmine?

FRED:    J-Jasmine? With all due respect, sir, this is the worst tea I've ever had. (*coughs up more tea*) This isn't tea. This is- this is seawater.

SIMON:    A bit harsh, don't you think? (*takes a sip and suppresses a gag*) You're right, this is seawater. (*writes down in notepad*) Reminder: Salt is the blue container. Sugar is red.

FRED:    (*Spits residue tea into cup*) Hopefully, the rest of this therapy session won't turn out as badly.

SIMON:    I'm a psychologist and not a tea maker for this very reason. Besides, you'll need to ingest at least 200 or so grams of salt for it to be lethal.

FRED:    Good to know.

SIMON:    Indeed. Now that was about 10 grams of salt, so try to avoid that stuff for a few days.

FRED:    Got it. (*dumps tea into potted plant*) No more salt.

SIMON:    (*dumps tea into potted plant*) Now that we've finished our lovely lesson on salt, how about some therapy? Start from the beginning, if you will.

FRED:    (*gathers himself*) It started last month.

SIMON:    (*flips to new page and starts writing*)

FRED:    I didn't really notice it at first. It was just minor things. The first few nights were just me ending up on the floor of my bedroom. I assumed I just rolled off or something. But, after a few days, it got worse. I started waking up in my kitchen, my living room, my bathroom. (*sigh*) It got even worse the next few days. I…wasn't limited to my house anymore. I started to go places. Like, really weird places.

SIMON:    Elaborate, please.

FRED:    One time, I was at a Justin Bieber concert. Then, I was at Donald Trump Rally. This other time, I ended up on a plane.

SIMON:    You were on a plane? What about airport security?

FRED:    Actually, I think it was a private jet.

SIMON:    Well then. That's… fascinating. Finish your story.

FRED:    After that, I knew I needed help. It keeps escalating, Doctor Freud. I don't know what to do. The last time I slept, I woke up on an Atlantic cruise. (*grabs SIMON*) Please, you have to help me. I don't want to end up on Mars. I just want to sleep and dream in peace. (*breaks down and cries*)

SIMON:    (*pats FRED's shoulder*) Now, now. Calm down. I can fix this.

FRED:    Can you, Doctor? Can you really?

SIMON:    Probably not. But you already signed the medical forms so, legally, I'm obligated to at least try. Lie on that sofa, would you? (*FRED stifles tears and lays on sofa*) Now, in order to determine the source of your problem, we need to go back. Back to any traumatic events that may have caused this.

FRED:    Like drinking your tea?

SIMON:    Mr. Darwin, I need your full cooperation on this, please. Just be as honest as possible. Can you do that?

FRED:    I-I'll try.

SIMON:    Good. Now, tell me about your mother.

FRED:    My mom. She's a sweet old gal. Raised me all by herself when my dad died.

SIMON:    How was your relationship with her?

FRED:    Like I said, she raised me all by herself. She pushed me to pursue higher education and take good care of myself. I guess she doesn't want a repeat of my dad. Can't blame her. She's been through a lot.

SIMON:    I see. What about your friends?

FRED:    I didn't really have any. I mean, I talked to people and stuff, but I'd never felt any connections to them. I mostly kept to myself.

SIMON:    This could be a potential source of your woes. Companionship is a great stress-reliever. Perhaps the sleepwalking is the subconscious yearning for the touch of another human being. In the light, you fear what you see, how others see you. However, in the shroud of darkness, of dreams, you are free. Your body longs for warmth. So it searches, a constant vigil against loneliness.

FRED:    (*looks beat*) Nah, I just don't like people.

SIMON:    Still, friends are good to have.

FRED:    I know. I had some in the past.

SIMON:    Ahh, we might have another clue. Pray tell, what is it. A scorned lover? A treacherous best friend?

FRED:    It's a guy I met at Summer camp. We were co-counselors.

SIMON:    That's not as exciting as my version, but go on.

FRED:    So anyway, Jason-- that's his name --Jason and I met at Summer camp. We got along pretty well. We would scare the kids together when we got bored. It didn't last though. We got into a fight toward the end of the camp. Left me with both eyes black, and I never saw him again. As in, my eyes were swollen shut, so I literally couldn't see him.

SIMON:    Ouch. Maybe this is your problem? You've failed the only meaningful friendship you've ever made. Sleepwalking may mean some part of you wants to rekindle the friendship with Jason.

FRED:    I don't think so. He was kind of a huge jerk.

SIMON:    Okay then. It's not people that cause you to sleepwalk. Perhaps it's something you ate. Have you recently had food that may be adverse to your health?

FRED:    Your tea.

SIMON:    Other than that.

FRED:    Not that I can think of at the moment.

SIMON:    (*thinks for a few seconds*) I'll cut to the chase, Mr. Darwin. You don't want to keep coming back here on a regular basis because I charge by the hour. And I have a lovely date with my secretary in the next hour. So if you please--

FRED:    --Wait, who are you going out with?

SIMON:    That's not important. The point is we both don't want to be here.

Therefore, with your permission, I will use my most powerful technique to cure you: hypnosis.

FRED: Hypnosis? Like the people who dangle a watch on TV?

SIMON: Exactly.

FRED: That works?

SIMON: You want to pay 100 dollars an hour talking to me every week?

FRED: Okay, I agree. Let's do this hypnosis stuff.

SIMON: Good. Sit up straight, will you?

FRED: (*straightens up*) So, how does this work?

SIMON: (*takes out a golden watch on a chain*) With this watch of course.

FRED: Really? I was joking about the watch. Shouldn't it be a pendulum?

SIMON: I could give you a sedative in tea instead?

FRED: I'm good. Watch swing is good.

SIMON: Look at this, will you? (*dangles watch in front of FRED*) Keep your eye on it. (*swings watch*) Let yourself relax. Let the sleep wash over you, like gentle ocean tides.

FRED: I'm not feeling it.

SIMON: (*say slowly and methodically*) Relax. Relax. Relax.

FRED: Okay, okay. I'm relaxed.

SIMON: Now, close your eyes. Embrace sleep's warm comfort. On the count of three, you will instantly fall asleep. One... Two... (*hits FRED with the watch, knocking him unconscious*) Three. (*takes FRED's wallet and exits left*)

(*blackout*)

*Scene 2*
(*In the same setting, with FRED out on the floor.*),

SIMON: (*enters left and notices FRED on the floor*) Oh--you're still here. (*prods FRED with his foot*) Wake up, Sunshine. I said wake up. (*Kicks FRED*)

FRED: Ow. (sits up)

SIMON: Oh good, you're alive.

FRED: What was that for?

SIMON: You were drooling on my carpet. It was custom made in Italy and costs a fortune to replace.

FRED: Did you have to kick me though?

SIMON: Yes.

FRED: Couldn't you--I don't know--bend down and whisper gently to me?

SIMON: I could've, but I didn't want to. I'm really full after my date you see. (pats his stomach) Don't want to pop the button.

FRED: You poor man. You must be in so much pain.

SIMON: Indeed.

FRED: As much pain as getting knocked out with a gold watch?

SIMON: Hey, it worked, didn't it? I reviewed the security footage before I came in. My cameras didn't show any peculiar activity while you were asleep.

FRED:      What on earth--

SIMON:     No need to thank me. Your money is enough. (*Tosses FRED his wallet*)

FRED:      You--you stole my wallet? (*checks wallet*) And my money too?

SIMON:     You were going to pay me anyway.

FRED:      I know, but it's the principle.

SIMON:     You're cured. That's all that matters.

FRED:      You could be arrested for assault, robbery, and malpractice, you know?

SIMON:     And I could slap you with my watch again. Blunt force trauma is much harder to cure.

FRED:      (*thinks*)You know what, Doc? I think that is a perfectly reasonable assessment. Thank you so much for your help. (*avoids SIMON's hand*)

SIMON:     A pleasure working with you Mr. Darwin. Do come back.

FRED:      (*nervous laughter, exits left*)

SIMON:     All in a day's work. (*sits back in chair*)

FRED:      (*enters left*) Did you take my ID too?

SIMON:     Oh. That. (*rummages through pockets*) I seem to have misplaced it. Sorry about that.

FRED:      (*turns to leave*) Wait. What would you need my ID for?

SIMON:     (*nervous laughter*)

POLICE:    (*off*) This is the police. Come out with your hands up, Mr. Darwin.

FRED:      What did you do?

SIMON:     Nothing too major.

FRED:      The police are here. What did you do?

SIMON:     I may or may not have brutally murdered my date and left your ID at the scene to frame you.

FRED:      Is that the truth, Dr. Freud? You're supposed to help me.

SIMON:     You going to jail helps me.

FRED:      No. I don't think I'm the one going to jail.

SIMON:     Hey, not my problem. It's your ID the police found.

FRED:      Because you left it there. Because you killed your date.

SIMON:     Yes, that's true, but don't make such a fuss. What's done is done.

FRED:      What is wrong with you?

SIMON:     Many things. I would know. I'm a certified psychologist.

FRED:      How? How could any sane human give you a degree?

SIMON:     Exactly. I wonder the same thing.

FRED:      Where did you graduate from?

SIMON:     St. Iscariot's School for the Criminally Reformed. I took a psychology class there.

FRED:      Then you admit you don't have a psychology degree. How? How are you working here?

SIMON:     The last doctor was a bore. And by bore I mean dead.

FRED:      So this isn't your first murder?

SIMON:     No, it is not. Don't be sad, Mr. Darwin. The police will personally escort you to jail.

POLICE: (*knocking loudly*) This is the police. Open up.

SIMON: Give prison a chance. Might be fun. (*shouts to police*) He's in here, officers.

POLICE: Open this door.

SIMON: Right away, sirs. (*opens door*)

POLICE: (*enter left*) Mr. Frederick Darwin, you're under arrest for the murder of Alice Cromwell.

FRED: Pardon me, officers. I do believe the man you are looking for is over there. I've held him as long as I could until you arrived.

POLICE: Our apologies, Chief.

SIMON: Chief? (*looking confused*) I'm his doctor. He confessed to the crime.

POLICE: Explain that to the judge, Dr. Freud, or should we say Mac Liniger.

(*Fred lunges at SIMON and pins him to the ground*)

SIMON: Now he's attacking me. Officer, if you will?

POLICE: Yes, we will Mr. Liniger. (*read SIMON his Miranda Rights and handcuff him*) You're coming with us.

SIMON: Excuse me? (*struggles futilely*) You have the wrong man. I'm Dr. Freud.

FRED: Right. And I'm Mr. Darwin (*shakes his head*). And if you hadn't hit me on the head (*rubs his head*), we would've had you sooner.

SIMON: (*in disbelief*) Then you double-crossed me.

FRED: (*smiling*) Survival of the fittest.

(*SIMON struggles*)

POLICE: Stop resisting arrest.

(*SIMON & POLICE exit left*)

FRED: Sweet dreams, Mr. Liniger. (*pours himself tea and takes a sip, then spits it out*)

(*BLACKOUT*)

FIN

# NOSTALGIA

I miss the towering sunflowers
Bright, yellow and larger than me
Petals decorating the heart of seeds
Cascading into a spiral of wonder

I miss the lush green grass
So soft it tickles bare feet
A special treat for pretend picnics
Completed with care free naps

I miss the deep blue skies
The warm summer's breeze
Gently hugging small shoulders
Cotton candy clouds drifting by

I miss the dog days
Hula hooping to the sway of trees
Snacking on delicious candy
Book after book engulfing me
Secret whispering instead of sleep

But most of all, *I miss you*

*Tiffany Leiterman*

# "SUICIDE IS ALL I'VE GOT" IS A LIE

Ah yes, of course
Betrayal
Consistently unexpected
Dare I say?
Extremely unavoidable
Frequent heartache
God, is this all there is?
Heart break upon heart breaks
I can't understand
Just how someone could enjoy this
Killing us all so slowly
Loneliness to the point of insanity
Mental disorder you say?
No one'll take you seriously
Overreacting, they say
Pathetic, they call you
Questioning people's intentions
Ruins your outlook on humanity
"Suicide is all I've got" is a lie
Think positively, please
Understand that you are loved
Vicious thoughts overflow
Will anyone miss you?
Yes, of course
Zealousness for life is still there.

*Noah Sabatini*

# IS THERE LIGHT AT THE END OF THE TUNNEL?

When darkness surrounds you,
Trapping you in all corners,
Making you lost in all directions,
Do you ever ask

Is there light at the end of the tunnel?

When everyone deserts you,
leaving the pain of loneliness inside,
Giving you the impression that no one loves you,
Do you ever wonder

Is there light at the end of the tunnel?

When you feel the sharp stab in your heart,
Hearing all of things that people think of you,
Bringing pain back into your mind,
Do you ever ask

Is there light at the end of the tunnel?

When nothing is going right ,
And it looks as though everything will continue to get worse,
Breaking your spirit down until it's gone,
Do you ever wonder

Is there light at the end of the tunnel?

When you tell yourself that everything will be okay,
Knowing that everything from here on out will not be,
Begging for your life to turn around for the better,
Do you ever ask

Is there light at the end of the tunnel?

When you hope for things to get better,

Forcing yourself to see the good in your life,
Demanding others to give you a reason to continue,
Do you ever wonder

Is there light at the end of the tunnel?

When you find yourself nearing the brink of death,
Remembering all the painful and joyful memories,
Wishing for things to have been different,
Do you eventually realize?

There is no light at the end of the tunnel.

*Tuyet Duong*

# LOOKING FOR THE LOST

Within my palms,
The shattered bits,
The ephemeral debris
Of a passion,
A motivation,
A life.

Within my hands,
The silent pleas,
The desperate yearning
For this passion,
This motivation,
This life.

Within my ability,
I manage only
The solemn memories
Of my inability.

I try to find,
To seek, to search,
To paste together those bits.
But all I discover
In the end is
My passion,
My motivation,
My life
Have ceased to exist.

*Monica Van*

# BARS, WALLS, AND A WINDOW

I came in and took a seat
surrounded by nothing but walls of concrete,
a window in front, bars on the side,
and a phone beside me.

Through the window
you saw me,
and I saw you
Both of us fighting tears; trying not to let it fall through.

But even through the glass
it still wasn't clear,
why you were in there
and I was over here.

How a person like you
could be barred up like this.
Out of all the people in the world,
you should be the last on that list.

We grabbed our phones and began to speak.
At first I couldn't speak,
but as always
You know how to get a smile out of me.

And for a while there were no walls, no bars, no windows.
It was us alone, talking
just like we would at home.
I had even forgot that I was holding this wired phone.

And just before our time was up
you said to me, "Don't let anyone take your smile away…
because you're the ray that shines on even the cloudiest of days."
And that's when I knew that you'd be okay.

*Emanuel Ramirez*

# I SEE YOU NOW

I see you now and I know you're questioning
Why your child won't grow up and figure out how to clean
His room the house the broken mess of his life
That isn't so broken as the one you left behind
I see you now and I know you're questioning
His choices his intelligence his interests his personality
Which is too feminine to be professional but too masculine to be girly
And have feelings and silence and sensitivity

I see you now and I know you're questioning
What might have driven such a bright child to suicide
What might have driven such a brilliant mind to subside
What might have driven such a broken life to want to die

I see you now and I know you're questioning
How your child feels more at home alone at 3am than in your arms
Or how your child won't look you in the eye when he says "I love you"
Or how your child lives with guilt and won't say a word
But finds it in himself to despise the world
That says he can't have long hair or stand with hands on his hips
Because he looks too much like a woman, or too little like a man

I see you now and I know you're questioning
Why you have never heard these thoughts but he writes this poetry
At one am two am three am because he is too ashamed
To let his hatred color his actions in the daylight where they might be seen
Or in his words and thoughts and feelings when you tell him he should be

something he is not but only because of filial piety

I see you now and I know you're questioning
Why I cover my mouth whenever it opens
because I want to hide the sharpened teeth that I made
to bite myself enough times to bleed out where nobody is dumb enough to help
why I give close lipped smiles instead of bright, sunny grins
to the warm faces you greet who I know as strangers that have stripped you away
to the world that stripped me of my individuality

I see you now and I know you're questioning
How I live with guilt and hate and resentment
How I still love and thank and am not relevant
How I think of death and life and a god
Who won't give me the time of day
But lets me live and scar and fade

*Dan Tran*

# A DUAL OF HONOR

The idea of
A duel of honor
has lost its touch today.
The smallest insult
Isn't so much.
Sarcasm,
has become the word of the land.
But when challenged,
I prepare myself.

Separated by a computer screen,
We prepare to fight.
We draw six cards.
For the first six turns,
We negate each other control of the game.
Then,
It comes.
A card of IMMENSE power.
only to get taken down
by a dwarf with a double-barrel.

Twenty minutes pass.
Both of us out of cards now.
Careful of every move we make.
Each time we draw,
We damage ourselves.
I have control.
But he has one spell on the field.
At his final life,
He draws.
The spell activates.
He remains alive.
My draw.
I lose.

A "duel of honor,"
Is what it's called.
But it was false.
It was only,
A duel to kill time.

*Richard Trejo*

# WINGS

My wings
Used to be beautiful
They reflected the light
Creating a rainbow wherever I went
Their small, white, fluffy form loved by all
But they were small

When they were small
I had barely enough to cover my selfish self
And people thought they were pretty
And that was enough

But then I found my friends
My friends began to change my wings
They grew as big as a whiteboard
Contrasting from one as well
Their black, jagged edges resembled coal
In order to keep those close to me warm

People say that it's ugly
It's selfish
It was better when I was younger

But I'd rather have these ugly wings
Than be alone, wrapping myself
with small, white ones.


*Nicole Le*

# LOVE LIKE A CHINESE RESTAURANT

Our first date was at a Chinese restaurant,
remember it?
The fortune cookies
we couldn't open
and the golden fish
that peered at us
through glass enclosures.

We drank tea out of
little porcelain cups,
and when it burnt your lips
I kissed the pain away.

The walls were this
deep red.
I thought,
"It's a close match,
but they still don't burn
as deep a red
as my heart."

For you
I was ablaze.
Every nerve and vein
lit a spark.

For you
I was a martyr
who died for the chance
to hold your heart.

I was everything
and anything
for you.

Sometimes I go back
to that Chinese restaurant.
The owners
walk down the aisles,
give a hello
and goodbye
to every customer
and every wanderer like me.

They recognize me now,
and ask where my love has gone.
My answer is always the same:
I'm still trying to find him.


*Sadie Adams*

# ABOUT THE AUTHORS

### SADIE ADAMS
Sadie Adams developed a love for writing and a particular fascination for poetry. Her favorite poem is "Ardella" by Langston Hughes. She will pursue writing in the future and hopes to eventually publish her own books.

### JENNIFER CHAU
Truly a child at heart, Jennifer Chau enjoys wearing pretty dresses, adorning flats shoes, and writing stories and poems. When she is not scribbling words on paper, she enjoys watching movies and making DIYs.

### TUYET DUONG
An aspiring author, Tuyet Duong spends her free time eating anything she can get her hands on. With the help of food and friends, she pushes herself to be the best writer that she can be.

### KEVIN HO
Kevin grew up influenced by animations of every genre, ranging from American cartoons to Japanese anime. His works were first published in "When You Give a Creative Writing Class a Deadline," and he continues to strive to create an original writing style.

### TRACEY HOANG
A lover of the arts, Tracey Hoang enjoys writing in her spare time. Although she may appear distant and cold at first, Tracey is a quirky and warm person at heart. When not writing, she enjoys listening to music, eating, and volunteering.

### ZACHARY KING
Zach King has always had a passion for adventure stories. Whether they were flying through space or exploring dungeons and caves, the characters he made always had strength and courage at their side, much like the man who wrote them.

### NANCY LE

Nancy grew up without any particular interest in writing, but after entering high school, she discovered a love for expression through storytelling, which lets her mind wander into unique places. Her first published work is "Lily's Legacy," and here she presents "The Blue Floral Door."

### NICOLE LE

Nicole Le is an aspiring author and artist, born and raised in Southern California. She is still a small meme, trying her best.

### BECKY LEE

Becky Lee is an abnormal teenager with an extra thumb, who spends her time eating, drawing, and writing late at night. She hopes to someday become a video game designer or writer.

### TIFFANY LEITERMAN

Tiffany Leiterman, having grown up in Huntington Beach, is fond of reading in the warm sun. Her reading hobby has extended to "creation bursts," which inspire her to jot down picturesque ideas for stories. Besides reading, Tiffany enjoys taking her black lab for long weekend hikes.

### CHRISTINA NGUYEN

Christina grew up with a love for fantasy and action. Her childhood consisted of reading fictional books, which sparked her interest in writing. Although she mainly writes short stories online, "Everything for a Glance" will be her second published work.

### GINA NGUYEN

Gina Nguyen has been a curious person since birth. She spends her time in life searching for flaws in the world and finding ways to neutralize them while she expresses her opinions and feelings through her writing.

### KARI NGUYEN

Kari Nguyen is a student who loves experimenting with different forms of art. Although she has always had a passion for writing, she was able to discover her true potential during senior year, when she took a creative writing class. Now, when not writing, she spends time creating artworks and watching YouTube videos.

### JENNY NGUYEN

Jenny Nguyen is a sleep-deprived junior whose hobbies include crying over fictional characters, illustrating fantasy worlds, playing romantic songs on piano, and reading angsty poetry. She usually writes in the dead of night.

### VINCENT NGUYEN

Vincent spends much of his time nurturing his love for fiction through reading, drawing, gaming, and (of course) writing. Although his ideal dream is to make choose-your-own-adventure novels, right now he is writing shorter prose for experience.

### HELLEN PHAM

Hellen Pham found friends who inspired and accepted her eccentric personality and she developed a love for drama and theater. She wants to pursue a career in criminology or teaching.

### THAOMI PHAM

By age four, Thaomi knew how to draw and color Hello-Kitty. Gate Art accepted her when she turned eight. She won 2nd place from The Imagination Celebration Art Exhibits and had "My Dad's Hands" published in the national anthology. She seeks to pursue a career in nursing.

### THONG PHAM

Thong Thien Pham -- eccentric, visionary, rebel. Ironically, he was quite adamant against writing, but with great books and greater teachers, he grew to love the art. He hopes to be successful in life.

### ALEXANDRA QUANG

Constantly craving fro-yo, Alexandra Quang is a student from the city of Westminster, California. She self-indulges in salt-n-pepper kettle chips, cat videos on YouTube, and writing her ideas on everything but paper.

### EMANUEL RAMIREZ

From Santa Ana, California, Emanuel Ramirez enjoys indulging himself in poetry whenever he has the chance. He hopes to continue writing poetry while studying to become a high school history teacher.

## MIKAYLA REILLY

Growing up in Westminster California, Mikayla Reilly thrived to find her purpose in life. Upon entering high school, she had loyal and caring friends who introduced her to the art of the fangirl. From that point on, Mikayla knew she only needed to do one thing: fangirl.

## ASHLEY RIVERA

Made in Southern California, Ashley Marilyn Rivera grew up in Garden Grove where she learned of art, reading, and writing. Although her original love was art, she soon discovered that she also loved the art of writing. Her first published work was "Jordan and Johnathan," and now she is proud to present her poem "He Sat."

## NOAH SABATINI

Noah Sabatini, the boy with a passion for anthropomorphic art, decided to broaden his creative expression by working on his writing skills in the Creative Writing class at LQ. Through lots of determination and frustration, he pours out emotional pieces of art representing himself.

## AISLINN STOLZE

Aislinn Stolze grew up in the city of Westminster, California where she discovered writing, art, and music. On most days she can be found writing, drawing, or hanging out with her friends. Her inspiration comes from her deepest feelings and experiences with her friends.

## MAGGIE TIEU

Maggie Tieu is a Vietnamese-Chinese student living under the harsh sunshine in California. Growing up with R.L Stine's "Goosebumps" series, she developed a strong interest in horror literature mixed with the right amount of humor. Outside of literature, she partakes in marathons of cartoons, whether old or new.

## ALLISON TRAN

Since middle school, Allison had a passion for badminton and volleyball. However, an injury forced her to quit both sports, leading her to begin writing about her feelings and personal experiences. She hopes that her works will resonate with others in the same situation.

## AMY TRAN

Amy Tran is an aspiring writer and hopes to major in psychology in the near future. She is a full-time Libra with the personality of a Pisces, who spends her spare time watching anime, listening to K-Pop, and freestyle dancing to EDM when time calls.

## DAN TRAN
Mobile gamer, idol enthusiast, and full time student, Dan Tran aspires to become a teacher and see a cat marry a tomato.

## YEN TRAN
Yen Tran is the oldest of eight children and has lived in California since birth. As an eccentric, her interests cover a wide range, and she is often open to new experiences. Peaches are great, but it seems she has a higher affinity for apples.

## RICHARD TREJO
Richard Kyle Trejo is a normal, teenage writer who has gotten into writing romance stories despite not being a fan. He knows that romance is not for him, but he can dream. His main YouTube channel is Wolf and Friends Gaming. Go support him.

## MONICA VAN
A Californian, Monica Van grew up in Santa Ana where she discovered her love for drawing, singing, and writing poetry. A few of her poems have already been published, and she plans to continually craft and to improve on her poetry.

## KIMBERLY VIRAMONTES
From Santa Ana, California, Kimberly Viramontes grew up loving to read and write. "You" is her first published poem. One day, Kimberly hopes to earn a degree in psychology.

## STEPHANY VIVAR
Stephany Michelle Vivar grew up between the border of Garden Grove and Santa Ana, where she discovered journeys and happy memories. She soon too enjoyed writing poems. The desire to write poems came to life when writing in her journal. "The Lonely Walk" is her first published poem.